Funfair
of fear

Ruth Morgan

Illustrated by
Chris Glynn

PONT READALONE

First Impression—2002

ISBN 1 84323 121 2

© text: Ruth Morgan
© illustrations: Chris Glynn

C/20 4/2014

This volume is published with the support of the
Arts Council of Wales.

Printed in Wales at
Gomer Press, Llandysul, Ceredigion SA44 4QL

For Gethin

Chapter 1

Bertie and Gertie

I was spending more and more time round at Uncle Wil's. Nobody at home seemed to mind. My sister, Avril, had just had her baby so Mam was up to her eyes in it. She was too busy to worry about what I was doing, as long as I was safe.

Wil, Mam's brother, used to live in an ordinary house in an ordinary street in Barry. Then he began collecting old bits and pieces from the local fairground. Before long 'Wil's Wacky Fun House' was offering free rides every day to local children. It was hectic but I loved it at Wil's place.

Wil and I shared a secret, too. He had been given two old bumper cars and the night after we painted them they had come to life! We suspected it was something to do with the old fairground paint we'd used. Anyway, one way or another, Bertie and Gertie were now more like pets.

Trouble is, have you ever owned a pet bumper car? Imagine a great lump of metal getting so excited it just wants to bump . . .

and bump

and bump!

It's lucky Wil is usually so patient.

Then about a month ago, to everyone's surprise,
Wil simply blew his top.

The four of us were watching *Star for Tonight* on telly when Bertie and Gertie started arguing.

Gertie wanted to vote for the man who could gargle jelly. Bertie thought the lady who played the xylophone with her feet should win.

That started them bumping each other, both clanking angrily.

'Careful, you two!' Wil was out of his chair.

But Gertie had taken a good swing at Bertie and . . . BUMP! He landed slap in the middle of the telly, which toppled over with a crash.

'There!' shouted Wil. 'Now you've broken the dratted thing and I haven't any money to mend it.' Turning to me, he said stiffly, 'Lauren, take them down the shed, where they can't destroy anything else!'

It was dark outside. I led the sorry-looking pair down the garden path and opened the shed door. I knew they hated it in there, with all those cobwebs.

'Don't worry,' I whispered, 'I'll talk to Wil. He'll come round.'

Gertie gave a clanky little sob as she shut the door and pushed the bolt across.

'They're really sorry, you know,' I began. I was stopped in my tracks. Wil was sitting at the kitchen table with his head in his hands. There were papers everywhere and those nasty brown envelopes Mam is always complaining about.

'Are they all bills?' I asked.

Wil nodded.

'But this one's dated four months ago.'

'I know.'

'And here's a red one. That means . . .'

'Yes,' Wil sighed. 'I didn't want to tell you, Lauren fach. We've used too much electricity. I've got no money to pay these bills. We're about to be cut off.'

And he started telling me about the terrible fix we were in.

Meanwhile in the back lane, a sinister looking van was lurking. A camera on its roof swivelled slowly around. As we later discovered, someone was watching the house that night and had spotted Bertie and Gertie making their way to the shed.

Chapter 2

Cut off!

Next morning, much sooner than expected, Wil switched the kettle on and . . . nothing. Then he tried the lights. Not so much as a flicker.

'That's it then,' he said sadly. 'We've been cut off. Lauren, what are we going to do?'

Wil's Fun House had been using much too much electricity, with all those rides and lights flashing on and off. If only Wil had charged his customers to go on the rides . . . But no, he simply hadn't thought of that. Wil was just too kind for his own good.

A sign appeared on the front gate an hour later. Before long, a sad crowd of children had gathered around it. This being a Saturday morning, they'd been looking forward to their usual rides and treats.

'What does it say?'

'Read it out again.'

WE ARE VERY SORRY
BUT THE FUN HOUSE
IS CLOSED TODAY.
WE ARE NOT SURE WHEN
WE'LL BE ABLE TO OPEN AGAIN.
WIL AND LAUREN.

'Out of the way, you little oiks!' Someone was pushing through the crowd roughly, someone dressed in a dark, flowing cape. He knocked several of the smaller children over with his expensive looking walking stick.

'Aha! Ahahahaha!' The man turned to a small, red-faced follower. 'What can it mean, Bootsie? Considering what we saw last night . . .'

'What was that, boss?' Bootsie asked dimly.

'The bumper cars, you twit!' the cape wearer hissed. 'I have to know how they can move like that, almost as if . . . they were alive. Think what it could mean for us. Come on, back to the van!'

It's a good job Wil and I knew none of this yet. We had enough to think about. The most important thing was paying those bills, and they amounted to hundreds of pounds.

In the end we came to a heart-breaking decision. Wil would have to sell off his fairground objects, all except Bertie and Gertie, of course. There was nothing else for it. Number Seventeen Windtop Avenue would have to turn back into an ordinary house once more.

Chapter 3

The Auction

An auction was being held at the Town Hall so we decided to take Wil's stuff along there. The large items, like the hot-dog stand, would be sold on their own but we thought it best to put the smaller items in crates and stick labels on them, giving an idea of what was inside.

Lots of our friends found out about the auction and turned up to support us on the day. Some of them said they wanted to bid, to help Wil out if they could.

Lot number thirty-five was the first of our sale items: a set of swingboats.

'Now, who'll start the bidding at thirty pounds?' asked the Auctioneer. A hand went up at the back.

'Thirty I'm bid. I'm asking thirty-five. Thirty-five? Thirty-five?'

Another hand shot up in the middle of the hall. It was Mrs Evans next door.

'What an earth will she do with them?' Wil whispered to me.

Mrs Evans turned round and winked in a friendly way at Wil.

'Never mind,' I whispered back, 'it might push the price up.'

The swingboats were sold for fifty pounds to 'the gentleman in the cape' at the back of the hall. It was a good start.

One by one all Wil's items were sold. Although there were times when I couldn't bear to look, I was adding up the sums and soon we'd made more than enough money to cover the bills. What a relief!

I turned around but Wil was nowhere to be seen.

'Mrs Evans, have you seen Uncle Wil?' I asked. She was on her way out.

'Sorry, lovely,' she replied. 'Hey, good though, wasn't it?' From behind her hand, she whispered, 'Lots of your friends here, pushed the prices up.' Wink, wink.

I thanked Mrs Evans and, after one walk around the hall, wandered out into the cool air.

There was a right old ding-dong going on in the yard outside. I hid myself around a corner and watched. The caped man, who had bought more or less all of Wil's stuff, was storming up and down, kicking the crates and thundering with rage.

'It's a load of old rubbish!' he yelled. 'It doesn't move. None of it's alive. What's in that crate, Bootsie?'

'Er . . . more mirrors, boss,' sniffed Bootsie.

'I can't believe I've paid so much for all this

junk!' He was spitting with fury. 'They were all
in on it, that lot in there. Pushing the prices up
deliberately.'

Bootsie was holding up a wibbly wobbly mirror.

'Look, boss, it's funny!' he chuckled. 'Can I
have it for my caravan?'

The Boss spun around and boffed Bootsie on
the head with his walking stick.

'No, you ninny!' he shouted. 'I'll be dumping
this lot, soon as I can.'

I was furious, too. Furious to see Wil's
priceless collection being treated so badly. And
what did the horrible man mean, 'None of it's
alive'? What was he expecting to find?

Bootsie started loading the fairground stuff into a dark van. On the side in flashy gold letters, was written 'Dr Snare's Travelling Funfair'. I turned away bitterly and went back into the hall.

Wil was there clutching a great wad of notes.

'Where did you get to?' I asked. I didn't tell him what I'd seen outside for fear of upsetting him.

'Well,' answered Wil with a huge beaming smile, 'we did so well at the auction, once the bills were paid there would still have been plenty left.'

'*Would* have been plenty left? What do you mean?'

Wil looked a bit sheepish.

'You've gone and bought something, haven't you?'

'Yes, but Lauren, what a beauty! Let me show you.'

And Wil took a photo from his pocket. It was a photo of a small, antique aeroplane.

'It's parked in the Flying Club in Rhoose. We're picking it up at five o'clock!' Wil beamed.

My heart sank but I couldn't tell him off. It was the first time he'd looked happy in days.

Chapter 4

The Invitation

Bertie and Gertie had spent the whole of that day in the shed again. They'd hidden when the removal men came and I'm sorry to say that when we left for the auction, Wil and I had forgotten to let them back into the house. It was later, much later, that I learned the whole story of what happened to them that night.

When it started growing dark, Gertie began getting restless. She wanted to undo the bolt on the door and take a look outside. Bertie tried to reason with her: what if someone spotted them? She knew they were never allowed out unless it was really dark.

Just then, a piece of paper slid under the shed door and they heard someone tiptoeing away.

Gertie pounced upon the paper. It was an invitation to a disco, promising 'Fun, Fun, Fun':

There was a map on the back of the invitation, showing the way to Dead End Field, just out of town.

Gertie was desperate to go but Bertie was dead against it. They argued for a good hour, by which time it really was dark outside. In the end Bertie couldn't stop Gertie. She unbolted the door and headed off with the map. Poor old Bertie had to follow: there was no knowing what kind of trouble Gertie might get into on her own.

Meanwhile, Wil and I had turned up at five o'clock to collect the plane. It looked even shabbier than it had in the photo and we spent the next four hours towing it home on a piece of rope tied to the back of Wil's camper van.

Every so often, we had to stop and pick up another bit of plane which had just fallen off. At last, when the second propeller went bouncing down the road, Wil hit on the brakes and we screeched to a halt. I gave him a sidelong look. He was sweating.

'Don't say it,' he mumbled tiredly. 'Just don't say it.'

Chapter 5

Kidnap at the Funfair of Fear

When they arrived at Dead End Field, Bertie was still pleading uselessly with Gertie to turn around and head back home.

The funfair was the kind that springs up overnight like a mushroom and disappears just as quickly. Strangely, though, that evening all the lights were out and no-one seemed to be about. The two little bumper cars wandered nervously between the empty rides and stalls. Here and there, mirrors gleamed eerily in the moonlight while strange faces decorating the rides seemed to fill the air with their horrible, silent laughter.

Then in the distance they heard music and spotted a gleam of light. Gertie headed off at once, followed by Bertie. As they got closer, they saw bumper cars hurtling around at great speed. Lights were flashing in time to the thumping disco beat. There was nobody in the cars but otherwise they seemed perfectly ordinary – not alive like Bertie and Gertie. Still, they seemed to be having a good time. Gertie joined in and soon even Bertie was boogying to the beat.

There wasn't much of a chance for them to enjoy themselves, though. Without warning the music and lights cut out and the other bumper cars slowed to a standstill. Gertie could hear Bertie panting beside her, worn out by all the dancing.

A single, very bright beam of light snapped on. It swept over the dance floor as though it were looking for something. Suddenly it hit upon Bertie and Gertie. The light was blinding.

'Well, hello!' boomed a deep voice. 'So glad you could join us.'

Gertie and Bertie bumped each other's bumpers, nervously.

'My name's Dr Snare,' the voice carried on. 'And this is my fairground. A bit grander than you're used to, I know. And now, I'm going to ask you both to come with me.'

Shapes were closing in on either side of them. Gertie and Bertie shot forward, hitting a man over as they went. The man was holding a net.

The fairground was like a huge maze and they couldn't slow down even for a moment to decide which was the best way to go.

'You can't get away!' yelled Dr Snare. 'We're right behind you.'

They came to a crossroads. By mistake
Gertie went one way and Bertie the other.

When she realised she wasn't being chased any more, Gertie slowed down and peeped back round a corner. She was horrified to see poor Bertie being dragged away in the net.

The caped man, who had to be Dr Snare, was rubbing his hands together.

'At least we have one!' she heard him laugh. 'A real living, breathing bumper car! The crowds will come flocking in! Throw him in the cage at the back of the Ghost Train.'

The men dragged Bertie roughly.

'Careful! Careful!' Dr Snare shouted. 'We don't want him damaged. When I return at midnight, the operation will begin. I'm going to open him up and find out how he works. When I've discovered that, we can make hundreds more like him.'

Bertie looked terrified and Gertie simply didn't know what to do. In a panic, she raced off in the direction of home.

About the author . . .

Is there a book you really love? For me as a child it was *The Lion the Witch and the Wardrobe* by C. S. Lewis. In those days my heroes weren't pop stars or sports stars, they were authors – and I wanted to be just like them.

I still have some of the stories and poems I wrote when I was six or seven years old at school in Llandovery, where I grew up. In the juniors I also started writing class newspapers. I tried to make them as funny as I could because I loved making my friends laugh. For me, the best stories have a funny side as well as something serious to say.

Hope you enjoy reading about Gertie and Bertie, Lauren and Wil!